FROM WINGS TO FINS

A Collection of Sapphic Fairytales

“From Wings to Fins: A Collection of Fairytales”
Written and Illustrated by Angela Flatt

ISBN: 979-8-9923256-9-0 (Hardcover)
979-8-9958017-0-2 (Paperback)

Listen to the accompany podcast here:

“AquaReal - Realistic Watercolor” brushes by Lisa Glanz
“50 Inking Brush Set” brushes by artbylouris
“Clouds Brush” pack by Devin Elle Kurtz

TABLE OF CONTENTS

Still For Michael

THE SIREN AND THE SUCCUBUS

Once upon a time there was a village. It was quiet and unassuming. The sort of place where one could grow up, start a family and die. But it was also the type of place where visitors only ever passed through. They never stayed, and they never remembered their time in the town. It was a simple life – not rich, not fulfilling, just simple. The people there could be described as content, but not happy. They did not leave, however, because it was all that they had ever known.

The only interesting thing about the village was the little house atop the highest hill in the deepest forest. Many of the villagers would spend their time whispering about this place. Some had tried to venture forward, to inspect it for themselves, but the stories about it filled them with as much fear as it did intrigue.

There was rumor that it belonged to a witch. A haggard, old woman who lured children to her doorstep in order to devour their flesh. Others said that it belonged to a Puritan, a woman so involved with God that she locked herself away to dedicate her time to worship. The truth was somewhere in between.

For inside the house on the hill in the forest, there lived a creature not from this world. One who would conjure herself into the dreams of men in order to feast. It was not out of malice that this act was performed, it was just the way her kind would feed. For she was a succubus.

She came to this village so long ago, to the point where no one in town could recall the house's construction. The succubus rarely found reason to leave her small haven. She was so old, and had devoured so many souls, that she only ever needed to come out once a year to feed. The rest of the time, she waited in solitude. A simple life.

The winter months that year were especially harsh. The chilled winds came early, and killed many of the crops before the harvest. The villagers became frightened that there would not be enough to eat, so it was decided that they must go out beyond the town and trade with other villages.

The winter months that year were especially harsh. The chilled winds came early, and killed many of the crops before the harvest. The villagers became frightened that there would not be enough to eat, so it was decided that they must go out beyond the town and trade with other villages.

Before the snows had a chance to settle in, the men of the town gathered together to board their largest ship. News of this adventure reached the succubus to her house. Nearly all the men would be aboard that ship, and out to sea where they would have no escape. It would be the perfect hunting ground for her.

Now the succubus had a human disguise. When she approached the ship, no one in the village recognized her. They assumed that she must have been a traveler, and she was so charmingly beautiful that they welcomed her to board.

What the succubus and the sailors did not know was that nearby lurked a siren. The aquatic creature was also ancient to this world. She had swam across many different seas in search for new prey. When she saw the men climb aboard their ship, she knew that it would be perfect.

This was not her trying to be cruel. Sirens were put on this earth to do one thing, and that was to cause storms which sank ships.

None the wiser to either predator, the men sailed out into the ocean. During the day, their time was peaceful. The waters were calm and the winds were strong enough only to push them forward. By night, however, it was quite a different story.

Once the men fell asleep, each of them began to dream about the beautiful woman who had come aboard with them. In their mind's eye, they saw what it would be like to hold her, to press their mouths on hers, to wrap their arms around her and pull her in close. The visions were so real that they could nearly feel her warm, soft body in their grasps.

But of course, this was all no dream. The succubus had entered their minds, and began to drain them of their souls. She continued her feast until a high pitched sound began to ring in her ears. It was an old song, one she had not heard since the dawn of time, but she remembered it all the same.

She ran to the edge of the boat to see what was happening. In the distance, she spotted the siren. The succubus felt helpless. She tried to call out to the other predator, but her cries could not be heard over the song's piercing melody. Thunder roared and lightning flashed as the storm this siren conjured picked up.

The ship rocked back and forth over the waves. One by one, the men fell out of the succubus's spell and under the siren's. They jumped over board, rushing past the succubus as they did so. All the while, the ship threw itself in every directions, until the succubus could hold back no longer and fell into the sea.

Immediately, her human disguise began to melt away, and the ocean's salty waters burned at her skin. It was so intense that smoke began to rise up where she was drowning. The sight of her caught the siren's attention.

It was an unfamiliar sight to be sure, but ancients recognize other ancients. The siren knew at once that the succubus did not belong in the sea. She knew that the succubus did not deserve to die by its waves. They had both been acting out of instincts.

So she dived into the waters and swam up to the succubus. The siren grabbed onto her and pulled the two of them above the surface. Without her singing, the storm calmed itself as the siren took the succubus to the shoreline.

Once they arrived, she set the firey predator down on the beach. The succubus did not stir. This worried the siren. It was difficult for her to crawl along the ground, but she did so in order to find branches and carry them back. The siren had seen stranded sailors before rub the sticks together to make fire, and that was what she did now.

When the flames finally began to spark, they popped out and burned at the siren, so that she jumped back. Yet she stayed put as the fire began to grow. The heat revived the succubus, who then sat up to look upon her savior.

The two were curious about one another. They had known about all the ancients in this world, but they had never seen the other in life before. Despite their differences, however, the siren and the succubus gazed into each other's eyes, and they knew one another.

They reached out to press their palms together, but as soon as their skin met, they burned one another. This revelation brought great sadness to them, because they had never longed to hold someone before tonight. Then the succubus had an idea.

She resumed her human disguise. The siren understood, and also dawned upon her own disguise. Now that their ancient flesh was concealed, the two reached for each other's hand yet again. This time, they were able grasp onto one another. Once they were able to embrace, they knew that they could never be separated again.

The succubus took her new companion back to the town. The villagers watched as the pair of strange women made their way passed the buildings and towards the forest. As they entered, bits and pieces of the ship's wreckage also came up to the shoreline. The town came in and gathered up the driftwood. Their fears heightened at the thought of winter and the men they had sent out to their deaths. They did not think these two arrivals were a coincidence. The charms which came from their human disguises were lost on the suspicious crowd. But with no evidence, they let them disappear into the trees.

The siren and the succubus were happy for a time. They often spent their days sharing stories from their lives, and all the things they had seen in the sea and in dreams. Then at night, they would dance under the stars. They found peace in not needing to hide their true nature from one another, even though they had to conceal their real forms underneath human skin.

One day, the succubus woke up to see her siren staring out the window. She was gazing longingly at the sea. The succubus knew that this arrangement would be harder on her lover than herself. After all, it wasn't as if the succubus could live under the ocean as the siren could adapt on land. It still pained her to see her beloved so full of melancholy.

She felt sympathetic, as well. She knew why her siren was staring into the sea today of all days. Both of them were becoming hungry.

But the siren could not feast on dreams, and the succubus could not enter the sea. So that evening, the two of them set off into town. Most of the villagers were asleep in their own homes, but there was one place where a small crowd of them still gathered. It was a place where men became drunken fools and where women earned their nightly keep. The siren and the succubus knew that their presence would go unnoticed in such a place, and that it would provide them with high quality prey.

All too soon, they stumbled across a man who was off in a corner. He was shouting at the woman sitting with him. She in turn was pushing him away, but the man would not comply. Just as he began to raise a hand, the siren and the succubus approached. They offered him what the woman refused. Now, the man remembered the day these two women came into town, but he was so drunk that his suspicions were dulled. He listened as they lured him outside.

Unbeknownst to the siren or the succubus, there was another villager watching as the scene played out. He was a man born into a cold world, and had lived a much more difficult life than most of the other villagers. His suspicions were higher than anyone else in town. He followed the three of them out the door and into the forest.

In the distance, he saw the dim light of a fire burning. He walked over, slow and careful, so as not arrouse their attention. Then he peaked through the leaves to witness a most unholy sight.

There were the two women, dancing around the fire, dressed only in the night sky. They sang in a language he did not understand. When they finished their dance, they embraced one another, their lips meeting as though they were husband and wife.

That was when the man spotted the most unholy sight of all. There, next to the flames and branches, was the corpse of the one they had brought out here. The man knew for certain then that these were evil creatures and had to be stopped. He ran back into town to warn the reset of the village.

When the sun rose the next morning, the siren and the succubus were asleep in bed together, content in their fullness. They bolted up from their drowsy daze as the door was bashed in. Before they could even fight back, the villagers came in and overpowered the pair. They took the siren and the succubus into the middle of town. A well waited to drown the succubus, and a pyre stood in wait to burn the siren.

As the crowd brought them closer to their fate, the two were torn farther and farther apart. They reached out for each other, longing to embrace one last time. The siren wondered how she could have ever missed her life in the sea, and the succubus wondered how she had ever spent so long alone.

Their time together had been so brief compared to the rest of their endless lives. Now it was over. Yet if they could do it all again, they would have chosen the same path. Whichever direction led to the other, they would have taken. They knew they would not truly be gone, only their flesh would be destroyed. A spirit never dies.

The last thing the succubus saw before the crowd threw her down the well was her siren being tied to the pyre. Smoke began to raise as she fell down. Lower and lower still, until she thought she might reach Hades before hitting the bottom of the well.

But she never reached it. Something grabbed her, and held her in place. Her feet fell against nothing, and yet she did not fall. There, she turned around to see who had saved her, and came face to face with her siren once more.

The two of them were dancing in the clouds, not in their human disguises, but as they truly were. Her siren was floating in her magnificent tail, which the succubus had not seen since the day they first met. As they continued to hold on, it dawned upon the siren that their touch was not burning one another. The two of them simply existed together, in pure honesty, up in the sky.

They came in closer and kissed. It was the most wondrous moment of their entire existence. Then all of it gently melted away, until the two of them were asleep in their bed once more. Their ancient flesh was shed once more, replaced with human skin. Yet these were not disguises. Their original bodies were destroyed, but now they were reborn as mortal women. No more need to hunt, no more need to hide.

It was just another day of them waking up to their life together.

THE FAIRY AND THE SPIDER QUEEN

Once upon a time, there was a fairy. She lived inside of a giant Venus Fly Trap, in the middle of the woods. Her life was care-free and happy. She spent her time tending to her great plant, keeping it healthy and full.

When the sun peaked up and the morning dew dripped fresh, the fairy would sing a little song. It was a soft melody which only the smallest of creatures could hear. But oh, how the insects of the forest would flutter over once they heard the singing. The fairy would lull them into her Fly Trap to digest.

There was only one shadow in her simple world. Up high in the trees lived a spider queen. She kept her web strung large and wide. Every morning, the spider queen would also sing, and her voice was so lovely that it would attract the insects of the forest up to her. This meant the fairy would have to sing louder and longer to retain her prey.

She wished that the spider queen would find another place to string up her web. But it seemed that she was more interested in stealing the fairy's haul rather than find food of her own. At least, that was what the fairy believed.

In truth, the spider queen knew that she could catch flies wherever she went. She was old, far older than any normal spider should be. She knew her voice was lovely enough to entice as large a meal as she desired. But it did not give her what she truly wanted.

And that was the fairy herself. She saw their singing as a duet, and thought of the fairy as her equal.

The spider queen longed for the day her song was strong enough to demand the curiosity of the fairy. She fantasized about the morning when she would sing, and the fairy would fly up to her web. On and on, they played this little game, and the forest was filled with their beautiful song. Yet the spider queen remained alone in her web.

Then one day, a great wind roamed over the woods. It was strong enough to make the trees bow and the bird's nests fly. It was strong enough to send the insects in all directions. It was strong enough to even lift up the fairy from the forest floor.

But the spider queen was old. This was not her first time experiencing a wind this strong, and she knew the secret to building her web to be stronger. So instead of panicking, she waited. She waited to catch the fairy as the storm blew her up towards her trap.

Once the fairy was caught, the spider queen wasted no time in securing her in. She tied down the fairy's wrists and ankles. She pressed her wings into the web so they were thoroughly stuck in place. Then she looked over her catch, pleased for the first time in several years.

The winds had been so strong that the fairy had become unconscious. She had no knowledge of where she was or what was happening to her. Eventually, her eyes opened, and she saw how trapped she had become.

The fairy cried and begged for the spider queen to let her go, but her pleas fell onto deaf ears. The spider queen had waited far too long for her prey to simply release her now. She reached down to the fairy's neck and sank her fangs into the soft flesh. The fairy's blood was the sweetest nectar the spider queen had ever tasted. There was the temptation to drink her fill, but she resisted. She wanted to make her catch last.

Days went by, and every morning the spider queen would wake up and sing their song together. She encouraged the fairy to join her, but their duet never returned. The fairy became dull and colorless. She seemed to be conscious less each day. Still, the spider queen would bite into her neck and drink.

Soon, however, the spider queen became sentimental. She longed for the days when she and the fairy would sing their hearts out to attract insects. Now that the fairy was trapped, she had lost all sense of life. So what purpose did the spider queen still have to exist?

She thought perhaps it would be best to let the fairy go. Let her resume her life of tending to her beloved Venus Fly Trap. Then they could continue their duet, and the spider queen would enjoy herself once more.

Yet when the spider queen went to unbind the fairy, she discovered that her prey was dead.

Where once she had found joy and desire, now lay only an empty husk. And that was all the spider queen's doing. She had no one to blame for this but herself.

She knew she could just pick up and go to another forest. She could start her life over. But what would be the point? Fairies were rare to come upon, and there was very little chance that she would find another like the one she had lost today.

The spider queen looked down to the forest floor, where her fairy's beloved Venus Fly Trap lay open. Its jaws were pointed and slick. Its mouth was wide, as though inviting her in. The spider queen found the call too difficult to resist. She took one last look at the fairy's corpse, and give its cheek a light kiss.

Then she leaped from her web and down into the Fly Trap. The last thing she saw before it clamped shut was the sight of the fairy, alone in her web.

THE FAIRY AND THE BAT

Once upon a time, there was a warlock. He lived in a castle atop the highest mountain, where no one would bother him and his study of magick. The only one he had around for company was his bat familiar. She had been with the warlock for years, and served him faithfully. Yet as time ticked by, both of them began to feel their youth fade.

The warlock became slow, but his patience grew thin. The bat started to lose her eye sight, and had a difficult time assisting the way she used to. This filled him with fury. He would throw things, and if he found nothing, then he would hurl the bat herself against the wall. He would yank at her ears and her wings, and he would call her ghastly names. It would make the bat miserable to see how badly she could upset her master.

There was still one job the bat was equipped to do well enough. At night, the warlock would set up traps for fairies, so he could harvest them for their magick. The fairies would glow so brightly that the bat had no trouble seeing them. As the sun set and the bat looked out the window into the distance, she spotted that familiar speck of light.

This night happened to be an especially bad one with her master. The warlock had been so rough with her that she had broken a wing. It was difficult for her to fly down to inspect the trap, but she knew she could not return empty-handed.

She spotted the trap and there was indeed a fairy captured inside. Perhaps the warlock would be so pleased with the bat that he would apologize for breaking her wing.

"Please," the little fairy begged as the bat approached her. "You must let me out!"

"I cannot," explained the bat. "For if my master were to find out, he would hurt me even more. He may even kill me."

"Why do you stay with him, then? If he is so cruel to you?"

The bat had thought this very question many times before. "Because I am his familiar. My place is by his side, that is my whole purpose in life. Besides...I have no where else to go. I don't have any other friends."

"I will be your friend," the fairy proclaimed. "If you let me out, I will become your friend, and I will stay with you until you are ready to leave."

These words softened the bat's heart. She leaned in closer to inspect the fairy. She hadn't noticed the details before, but now that they were next to one another, the bat could see that the fairy was truly beautiful. The most beautiful creature she had ever seen.

But the bat was cautious. She knew that fairies were known for trickery and deceit.

"How can I trust that you won't run away once I let you out?"

The fairy held up one hand. "Let me heal your wing now. Then you will know that my words can be believed."

The bat agreed, but she did so reluctantly. She knew that if her master ever found out about this deal, he would be awfully upset. But she could not serve him without a proper wing, and he would be upset regardless. So she held out her wing and allowed the fairy to take hold.

The fairy's touch was the softest the bat had ever experienced. Her grip was as light as air. The bat tried to recall the last time someone had held her for comfort. There was a tingling sensation in her wing, but it did not hurt. It was followed by a bright glow, and the pain was gone. In fact, the bat suddenly felt better than she ever had in her life. As though every ailment inside of her had been fixed at once. A deep warmth resonated inside of her.

"I have done as requested," the fairy replied. "Now will you please release me."

The warmth inside of the bat dissipated with these words. She shrunk down, afraid of what the fairy would say if she was rejected. But she had indeed held up her end of the bargain, and the bat wanted to be fair to her new friend. She opened up the trap.

"You must leave quickly before the warlock sees you," the bat warned. "He may have already sensed the magick you used to... to heal me..."

The fairy stepped out of the trap. For a moment, she looked out past the trees and into the sky. As though she was contemplating on leaving. Then she turned to the bat.

"We are friends now. And I will not leave a friend."

The two of them headed for the castle, around the back way. This was to avoid arrousing the warlock's suspicions. From there, the bat took the fairy into her little room. Actually, it was just a hole in the corner of the wall. It was plenty space enough for both of them, however.

The bat did her best to be a gracious host, even though this was the first time a guest was staying in her room. She laid out extra blankets for the fairy to sleep on. Then she brought out her supply of fruit, in case her new friend became hungry.

Then the bat curled up to go to sleep. "Good night, sweet fairy."

"Good night, dear friend."

And so this was their routine for a time. The bat would get up when the warlock did, and tend to her duties. She did not know what the fairy did with herself while they were apart. The bat's only warning for her was to remain out of sight.

Then after sunset, the two would curl up in the bat's little room. They would talk for a while, sharing stories, and the fairy would sing lullabies. The bat could not think of a time when her life had been happier. Even though she still spent her days working for the warlock, and even though he still mistreated her, she found that things weren't as bad as when she had been alone.

When the bat would return to her room, the fairy would heal the wounds inflicted upon the bat that day. Then she would ask again for the bat to leave with her. But the bat did not want to evoke the warlock's wrath. The fairy was powerful, however the warlock had drained many fairies.

If they ran away, he would come looking for them. Even though the bat was old now, he would not want to lose what belonged to him. They would always be running. She could not inflict that life upon her friend.

Every night, the fairy would ask, "are you ready to leave now?"

And the bat would respond, "good night, sweet fairy."

"Good night, dear friend."

This carried on for some time more. Until one night when the fairy trap became full once again. The bat found herself conflicted. She knew that the fairy would demand for the release of her kin, but she also knew her master would not take kindly if he discovered her second betrayal.

So she asked the fairy, "would you leave me, if I let him drain this fairy? To protect you?"

"I am your friend," the fairy answered, holding up her hand. "I have sworn to remain by your side."

The bat felt relief at these words, but only temporarily. For when she went down to the trap to recover the catch, she found that she could no longer only see an energy source for her master. When she looked at this new fairy, the bat thought of her friend.

More than that, she saw a small creature who was helpless and trapped. The bat saw herself.

Then she let this one go, as well.

"Fool!" Screamed a voice behind her. The bat did not need to turn around to know that her master had been watching. "I knew you were betraying me! My traps never fail!"

The warlock was so infuriated by her actions that he beat the bat within an inch of her life. He left her there to die.

Then he returned to his castle to search for the fairy he knew his familiar had kept in the castle. He had always known — fairies cannot hide their presence. Flowers had begun to bloom around his fortress, and the storms or winter winds never came anymore.

He had always known. He had simply waited for the right moment to strike. The fairy would be weakened from healing his familiar every night, but her strength could be renewed after he captured her and took the magick for himself.

He knew exactly where his familiar liked to sleep, so it did not take him long to find the fairy. She herself was napping, and unaware of the eyes on her. When the warlock saw her, he became enamoured by her beauty. She was the loveliest creature he had ever seen, and it was almost a shame to drain her magick.

The warlock thought of his familiar, left out to die, and how he will need a new companion by his side. Perhaps he could fashion a different use for this fairy.

He was gentle in lifting her up, so as not to disturb her slumber, and carried her off to his study. There he used what was left of his magick to transform the fairy into a human girl.

It wasn't until the spell was complete that the fairy woke up and realized what was happening.

"Where is my friend?" She asked, but the warlock gave no answer.

He told her that if she ever wanted to be a fairy again, she would have to first marry him and swear to be by his side until his death. The fairy cried, but in this human form, she had no magick left to defy him. She agreed to his terms.

Meanwhile, the bat remained at the bottom of the forest. She knew her fairy friend was in trouble, but she could not get back up to help her. She laid on that ground knowing that she would die. She thought about how every night her fairy would ask if she was ready to leave, and every night the bat had refused. She thought she had been protecting her friend. In truth, she had just been afraid.

And now they were both in mortal danger. The bat closed her eyes and began to weep.

Just then, she heard a fluttering sound. It started low, but became louder and louder. It was the sound of fairies in flight. Dozens of them.

The bat opened her eyes as one landed next to her. Even with her foggy eye-sight, the bat could see that this was the fairy she had rescued that morning. She had returned with an army to help the bat.

The fairies gathered around and summoned all of their magick. They not only healed the bat, they transformed her. She felt her body grow in strength and in size. At first, she thought that she was becoming human, for her legs expanded, and arms protruded past her shoulders. Then she noticed that her wings and claws remained. She was now a gargoyle.

Her eye-sight was healed, and she had the stamina to fly back to the castle. Which is exactly what she did. With her new size and fairy army, she stormed the stoned walls. She flew down the hallways with great speed, until she made her way to the warlock's study.

There she found not her fairy, but a human girl. One in a long dress who was prepared for a matrimony ceremony. Yet her transformation did not fool the gargoyle. They both recognized one another immediately.

The warlock appeared. He tried to attack the gargoyle, but he had used all of his magick. He was now just a withered old man.

"No!" He shouted as the gargoyle approached him. "You belong to me! Bat or gargoyle, you are my familiar! And you will do as I command!"

The gargoyle shook her head. If she had years to do so, she could not say all the things she had wanted this old man to hear. It did not matter. She did not need to waste a single breath on ears which refused to listen.

The gargoyle easily overpowered him. Even though she felt that he deserved to suffer, she could not bring herself to prolong his pain. She grabbed his head and tore it off. The army of fairies hovered over his corpse and set it on fire, turning him into ashes.

Now that this threat was out of the way, the gargoyle approached the human girl. Even while concealed in human flesh, she was still the most beautiful creature the gargoyle had ever seen. She was afraid at first that the girl might not want to embrace her. The gargyole was used to being small and helpless. She still did not know how to direct this new power she beheld. Her fears were assuaged when the girl took hold of her claws.

"Can they change us back?" The gargoyle asked, referring to the fairy army. She did not know why this was the first question to come to her mind.

The girl did not answer. Instead, her reply was, "do you want to change back?"

The bat thought about her old body. How it had been abused for years. Now she was in new flesh, one which had never been beaten by the warlock.

"No." She answered honestly, but then she noticed how the girl's face fell at her words. It frightened the gargoyle, but then she had another thought, and asked "do you?"

"Yes, but..."

"What's wrong?"

The girl bit her lip. "I'm worried about being so much smaller than you now. When you were a bat, we were the same size."

"Why should that matter?"

"I am worried that if I am so much smaller, you might not want to be with me. For you are more than my friend. I love you."

Then for the first time, the gargoyle smiled. She was reminded of the warm feeling she had back when the two of them had first met. "Why would you think that your appearance would matter to me? Don't you know I love you back?"

The two embraced, and shared a kiss before the fairies gathered around and restored their sister. She was now small enough to fit into the palm of the gargoyle's claws. But it was fine, because they were both in the bodies which made them happy.

So the fairy asked once more, "are you ready to leave?"

And the gargoyle answered, "let's go, and never return."

THE BUTTERFLY AND THE MOTH

Once up a time, there was a butterfly. She considered herself to be a very lucky butterfly indeed, for she lived in a greenhouse. It was always summer where she lived, no matter what the weather outside looked like. There was an endless supply of beautiful flowers to drink from. She also had a big family of butterflies to play with.

This was how they spent their days — the butterflies would wake up, have some breakfast, sing in their choir, dance, have some lunch and a nap, and then spend the rest of the afternoon with free time. It was a blissful existence.

At night, the butterfly would stay up later than the others to watch the stars come out. She liked to make pictures of them in her mind, and would tell herself stories about their lives. She wondered what might it be like to be up in the sky and watch all of the world. Sometimes the butterfly would press against the glass of the greenhouse, and ask herself what life was like beyond its barrier.

What did snow feel like? What did rain feel like? What did wind feel like? What other plants grew out in the wild? What other animals existed?

"Don't ask questions like that," the other butterflies would jeer whenever she brought up the subject. "We are safe inside the greenhouse. We are comfortable. Insects out there face threats like birds or poison. We can live peacefully away from all of that. You should be happy."

The butterfly was indeed happy. She liked to sing and dance. She just also wondered what else was out there. Mostly, she wished for a friend who understood her thoughts.

Eventually, the butterfly stopped asking so many questions. She would pretend to fall asleep the same time everyone else did, then secretly sit back up to look at her stars. One night, the butterfly noticed a star that was shining especially bright. She thought this might be a wishing star. She clasped her hands together and said the magick words.

"Starlight, star bright, first star I see tonight. Wish I may, wish I might, have the wish I wish tonight. I want a friend. Someone who understands me."

The star twinkled, as though it was winking at her. The butterfly smiled, thanked the star for listening, and went to sleep. Some time later, she was awoken by a rustling sound.

She sat up, wondering what it could be. She looked around to see if any of the others had woken up, but they all remained in blissful sleep. So the butterfly went up to the window for inspection.

Outside, she saw a group of moths flying around. They seemed to be attracted to the stars and their light source. They were dancing in a way which the butterfly had never seen before. The dances she and the other butterflies performed were choreographed and well rehearsed. The moths seemed to move completely at random, as though they were making up the steps as they went along. It looked like a mess, however, they all seemed to be having fun.

There was one moth in particular who separated herself from the rest of the group. She flew higher up and closer to the stars, so that she was eclipsed by their light. She appeared to be glowing. It was the most beautiful sight the butterfly had ever seen.

Just then, she noticed the one moth was coming closer. The butterfly felt anxiety rise inside of her. She worried what the moth might think if she saw her, but the butterfly could not explain why she cared so deeply. Perhaps she should pretend to be asleep. Yet as the moth drew in, and her features became clearer, the butterfly found that she could not take her eyes off of her.

Soon, the moth was at the glass. She pressed up against it, and the butterfly did the same. She wished to break past it so she could greet the moth. She felt her cheeks turn hot at the thought, as though her thoughts could be read. Yet the moth only smiled.

She moved her lips to imply that she was speaking, however the glass was too thick for her words to pass through. So she blew on it to make a cloud with her breath. Then she drew little dancing stick figures into existence. The butterfly thought she understood — she hoped she understood — that the moth was asking her to come out and dance with them all. The butterfly nodded, but she had no idea how to leave the greenhouse.

The moth appeared to be thinking as her eyes surveyed their parameters. Then she flew back over to her group of friends. This made the butterfly despair. She thought that perhaps the moth found their situation too difficult and gave up altogether.

She perked up, however, when she saw the other moths join hers in returning to the butterfly's side. Her moth motioned for her to get up, which the butterfly did, and she joined the rest of the group in their spontaneous dance.

At first, the butterfly was nervous. She kept wondering if she was doing it right, and found herself dancing the way she had been taught out of habit. But the moths did not seem to mind. Her moth kept coming closer to the glass, and would move slow enough for the butterfly to catch on. Soon, the two were dancing in tandem with one another.

The butterfly felt a strange sensation in her stomach. She didn't have words to describe the fluttering happening inside of her. Was this what happened when someone made a new friend? Is that what she and the moth were now — friends? The butterfly thought she might like that very much.

It seemed as though an instant had passed before the sun came up and the moths dissipated. But her moth stayed behind just a little longer. She blew on the window again, and drew into the fog the shape of a heart. The butterfly did not know what this meant, but she felt her own heart quicken in pace.

She hoped that the moth would return the following evening, if nothing else. The day carried on for an eternity to her. She had never realized how boring and monotonous her life was before the moths had come. How she and the other butterflies sang the same song and danced the same dance every day. She tried to find the joy she had once felt in her routine, but she simply felt none.

When the day at last came to an end and she sat by the window to watch the sun set, the butterfly wondered what it would be like to hold her moth. Would she be soft? Would her feathers tickle? What did her voice sound like?

Maybe one day, the butterfly would find out.

The sun stretched once more before disappearing, and the stars filtered throughout the night's sky. She watched in anticipation as the other butterflies laid their heads down to sleep. Then she continued to watch until the familiar pack of moths swarmed down to her greenhouse.

Her moth approached immediately. The butterfly leaned in close to the glass and blew on it. Then she drew her own rendition of the two of them dancing together. This made the moth smile, and she began to pose. The butterfly stood up as well, and into the night the two of them danced.

All the while, her moth looked so beautiful in the moonlight. The butterfly started to wonder what kissing her would feel like.

The next morning, the other butterflies tried to wake up their sister, but she would not arise.

"Is she sick?" They asked. "How could she possibly be sick? No one has ever been sick in here before."

The butterfly turned over and told them that she was merely tired from stargazing so late. She had never lied to the rest of them before, but she worried what they would think if they discovered her new moth friends. The other butterflies seemed to accept her answer, and warned her not to stay up too late again. It would be a shame if she missed out on their routines.

The butterfly could not be bothered with their worries, though. She slept that day and dreamed of night, of moonlight, and her beautiful moth. She was so caught up in her ecstasy, that she failed to notice that the others around her had started whispering.

They were worried about their sister, and that her deviation from the norm would cause trouble for their idealistic lives. So that night, they decided to feign sleep, and watched to see what it was their sister was really doing.

That evening, when her moth reappeared, she drew something new against the window. It looked like a door being open. The butterfly understood at once, but the realization brought her great anxiety. The moth was asking for her to leave the greenhouse.

The butterfly tried to mitigate. She gestured towards the greenhouse as a means to invite the moth inside. But her moth shook her head, and pointed at the drawing of the door. The butterfly sighed. She didn't know what would happen if she agreed.

How would they even get the door open? Would she be able to get back in? Would her family let her back in? Would they be able to close the door? Would she ever be able to leave again?

The butterfly thought about the first night she and the moth had danced together. How afterwards, her usual way of dancing had felt so boring. And no matter how hard she tried, she just could not enjoy it the same way she had before. She wondered if she left the greenhouse tonight if she would ever even want to go back inside again.

But then she looked at her moth. All of her thoughts began to swirl together. How the butterfly had longed to hold her, to hear her voice and dance by her side without the glass between them. If she did not do this now, she may never find the courage to do so.

She nodded her head. Her moth pointed to the real door of the greenhouse. All of them flew over to it for inspection. The handle would be easy enough for the moth gang to push down on, but it was locked from the inside. The butterfly would have to turn it open herself.

She reached out to do so when —

"Don't!" Cried her family. "The dangers are too great! You will expose the greenhouse to all the evils of the outside world!"

The butterfly pulled away. Her family stayed back, out of fear for the door, but she knew it would only be a matter of time before they flew over to take hold of her. They would never allow her to sit up during the night ever again. They would never let her dance with her moth again, let alone meet her.

She didn't want her decisions to affect her family. She just wanted to dance with her moth. She stared out of the glass and into her moth's eyes. The butterfly tried to remember happiness before meeting her, but the memories were hazy. All that came to mind was the moth's face.

She could not live without her.

So, the butterfly unlocked the door.

Her family cried out once more as the moths pushed down on the handle. The door opened with a burst of wind, knocking back all the butterflies and a few of the potted plants. For the first time ever, there was a chill within the greenhouse. All was silent.

The butterfly gathered herself. For a moment, she thought to herself "what have I done?" Someone could have gotten hurt from her reckless actions. But there was no turning back now. Even if they managed to close the door, it would never change the fact that she had opened it in the first place.

She brushed off her wings before attempting to stand up. Then, someone held out a hand for her. She looked to see her moth, waiting there, no glass between them.

The butterfly was hesitant, as though this were a dream and her actions would dissipate it. Eventually, she took her moth's hands. They were indeed as soft as she had always imagined. The two stood there together, gazing into each other's eyes before fully embracing.

Warmth filled the butterfly as she pressed herself into her moth. Her happiness was so strong that she thought she would cry from it. The guilt she had felt just moments ago was gone, as she knew that she had done the right thing.

Then the two of them looked around and saw that the other butterflies had

had started talking to the moth gang. No one had been injured, and so the panic had melted down into curiosity. The butterflies began to sing their songs, and the moths started to dance spontaneously.

That was when the butterfly and the moth knew that they were free to be together.

The butterfly turned back to her moth, and spoke her first words to her, "I love you."

And her moth spoke back at last by saying, "I love you too."

THE MERMAID AND THE SIREN

Once upon a time, there was a mermaid. She was smaller and shyer than most of her kind. While others liked to venture out into the world, she preferred to stay in her room and watch the many creatures which swam by. Most merfolk enjoyed approaching the surface so they could sing to the sailors, but not this particular mermaid. Because she had no voice to sing with.

There had been a time many years ago when she had possessed the most beautiful voice in the world. She used to sing for hours, entrancing not only the humans above, but also other merfolk. They would gather for miles just to hear her voice.

Then one night, she had been out a little too late, and a group of orcas had appeared. It was common knowledge that orcas did not care for mermaid voices, and saw them as competition. The other merfolk had all fled, but our mermaid had not moved fast enough, and one especially bold orca came and grazed its teeth against her vocal chords.

She had managed to escape after that. Everyone was relieved that she had survived. They often told her that she should be happy to still be alive. But everyday she awoke to the scars on her throat, and the memory of the voice she once had.

The mermaid lived alone with her mother, who did everything in her power to take care of her daughter. The mermaid had to learn sign language in order to communicate. She would often sign out her own poetry, and her mother would recite it back to her. In that way, she was still able to express her soul.

The two of them got by, more or less. The mermaid was grateful that she had someone in her life who loved her so much. She often lied awake at night and wondered what life might have been like if she had never been attacked. She kept just how much she was hurting inside to herself however, because she didn't want her mother to feel like she wasn't doing enough.

Then one day, there was a rumor spreading about that a siren had come to town. Sirens were different from mermaids. They lived much deeper in the ocean, and their skin was made of scales instead of flesh. They also did not use their songs to entertain others — instead, they used them to lure sailors into the sea and cause storms.

Siren voices, unlike mermaids, did not attract predators. If anything, it acted as a repellent. A warning that a much greater threat was nearby.

Merfolk generally tried to avoid sirens, but they did nothing to drive this one away. The rumor was that she had come to sing a concert. It would be so deep in the water that no ship would be able to hear it. The town found this intriguing — a siren who wanted to sing for fun?

Even the mermaid's mother expressed an interest in going. "It's just such a novelty, who knows if we'll ever see something like this again?"

The mermaid wanted to refuse. To her, the concert would serve only as a reminder of what she once had. She could foresee it being a night where she rubbed at her scars with great fervor. However, she wanted to let her mother have this. She had done so much for her over the years, she deserved a night of wonderment.

Her mother did not feel too keen on leaving behind her daughter, but the mermaid had insisted. So when the sun began to set, her mother set off into the depths. Soon the moon cast its light from beneath the surface, and the mermaid found herself watching its beams as they danced. She wondered if this was how the rest of her life was going to be. If one day she would be old and still unable to listen to the singing of others without feeling a profound sense of loss.

That was when she heard it. The singing. The concert must have just started. The mermaid grew worried about the fact that she could hear it, even so close to the surface. The siren had assured everyone that her voice would cause no storm. Yet as the mermaid went to cover her ears, she found that she could not resist listening.

It was the most beautiful voice she had ever heard. But it was not just the singing which captivated her, it was also the lyrics. The siren sang of a broken heart after losing her love.

"After all the years which have passed by,

Still on and on my heart does cry

For you were always a part of me

And now I am alone in the sea"

The mermaid felt a pang inside of her chest. She touched at her throat. She had no idea who or what the siren was singing about, but in the mermaid's heart, she felt a connection. Was it possible that the siren understood such things?

She wanted to go out and get a better listen, but she feared how she might react. What if the memory of her attack was too great? What if her heart broke completely in two?

Then a new thought entered her head — would refusing to listen bring her voice back? Would living with this fear bring her voice back? Of course the answer was no. So why should she be afraid?

The mermaid swam from the cave. The waters became cold and dark, and she felt exposed out there in the open. But she pressed on. Soon enough, she came upon the crowd of merfolk. In the center of the gathering, was the siren.

She was much larger than any of the merfolk. Her scaly flesh glistened in the dim light, making her shine. Her hair stretched out for miles, looking like a storm all on its own. She was a magnificent and terrifying sight to behold.

And her voice was captivating.

The mermaid swam in closer. She felt as though the rest of the world had simply vanished, and the only real things left were now her and the siren. Never once did she think to touch at her scars as she took in this frightening beauty.

Her lyrics once more reflected sorrow and heartbreak. They seemed to reach out and touch the mermaid's soul. Then the mermaid did something she hadn't before. She began to sign. Her hands moved in rhythm and sync with the siren's songs, as though the two were sharing a duet.

This strange sight caught the attention of those nearby. Soon, the audience had turned to see the little mermaid who was signing the siren's songs. But the mermaid hadn't noticed their looks. It was only when siren had suddenly stopped her song that the mermaid realized the attention she was attracting. Embarrassed, and she folded her hands behind her back.

But the siren only smiled. She reached out her hand, "come here to me, please."

The mermaid did as she was told, not knowing if there was another choice. Her stomach flipped inside of her, and she started to wish that she had never come here in the first place. However, the siren was so beautiful, and her song had filled the mermaid with such emotion, that she felt compelled to join her in front of everyone.

"What is your name?" The siren asked.

The mermaid spelled it out with her hands. The siren nodded. Then, much to the mermaid's surprise, the siren began to sign back.

'Can I tell you a secret?' The siren asked with her hands. The mermaid nodded. 'I used to be the most feared siren of the sea. Ships would avoid my waters just to evade my hypnotic song. But one day there was a sailor who was very brave and very foolish. He tried to kill me, but instead he only took my ears. I have not been able to hear my voice ever since.'

The mermaid gasped in surprise. The siren could not hear how lovely her song was? How had the sorrow not consumed her?

'Why do you still sing then?' The mermaid asked. 'Does it not cause you great pain?'

The siren answered, 'of course it does. I miss my voice everyday. But it would cause me greater pain if I did not sing at all.'

The mermaid felt her spirit move at the siren's words. It was as if something broken inside of her had mended. Not gone away, just stitched back together. Then, for the first time since her injury, the mermaid felt like singing.

She signed her lyrics to the siren, who in turn began to sing them. She matched every note and melody, as though she could hear the song in her mind as clearly as the mermaid heard it in hers. The mermaid thought about how every thing which had happened to her had culminated into this moment, of her and the siren creating music together. And she wouldn't have it any other way.

The two carried on their concert. The other mermaids were amazed by them. They listened well into the night, until the moon vanished and the sun came up once more. The mermaid and the siren carried on their concert the following evening, and the one after that, and even after that as well.

Once every mermaid in their area had heard their songs, the pair moved on to other parts. They swam from ocean to ocean, singing and signing. They wrote songs about their sorrow, their pain, but mostly, they wrote about they renewed joy and hope.

Then one day, the mermaid had prepared a special song for her siren. She would not tell her what it was about. She instead made the siren wait until that night. The siren was nervous about singing a song she did not know, but she trusted her mermaid.

Once the moon was performing its nocturnal dance, and the pair found themselves alone. The siren looked at the mermaid expectantly, and she began to sign her lyrics.

"You alone have mended my heart

You alone have given me this new start

You alone are the one I want at my side

Through the waves and through the tides

For you alone made me know,

That I am not alone

It's you alone I want, and you alone I need

So you alone I'll ask, will you marry me?"

LOVE POTION

Once upon a time, there was a kingdom. It was ruled by a horribly cruel king, and his equally cruel queen. They treated their subjects with malice, but no one received their wrath more than their staff. The men and women of the court lived in fear everyday. They would speak in quiet voices and never bring up strife, for they worried what the king and queen might do to them and their families.

The most scared of all were the servants who worked in the kitchen. The king and queen were notoriously picky eaters. They would fuss and fight if any part of their meal was not cooked to perfection. The kingdom had seen many chefs slaughtered for their perceived negligence.

Their latest chef was a young woman. She had never wanted to be hired onto the royal court, but someone had to feed the king and queen. She felt that it might as well be her. She did what she could to stay out of trouble. She took great care in knowing the preferences of their rulers. How the king liked his steaks rarer than the queen. Or how the queen enjoyed larger quantities of salt than her husband. More than anything, the young woman took note of what they drank. The kind preferred white wine, while his wife preferred red.

One night, while the young woman was preparing their dinner, she made a horrifying realization. There was no more wine in the castle. She searched all over, and when she could not fine any, she called for grapes to be brought. Yet none were ripe enough to pick. The young woman wracked her brain, until she recalled a rumor she had once heard.

Legend had it that there was a secret wine cellar within the castle. The servants said that the queen was more fond of red wine than she let on, and went out of her way to import it from distant lands.

The young woman wasn't certain if she believed these rumors, but it was worth a shot. She took forth and rummaged around the kitchen. She turned over empty shelves, placed her hand along the stones in the walls, and checked under the rugs. At last, she came upon a hidden compartment.

Without a second thought, the young woman lifted the latch and stepped inside. Relief washed over her instantly as she looked around and discovered a cellar full of red wine. The bottles came in many different shapes and sizes. The hue of the wine was the deepest, purest form of the color she had ever seen. It sparkled like a ruby.

She reached for a bottle. She told herself that she needed to make her way back upstairs quickly, yet something held her in place. She found that she could not take her eyes off of the bottle in her hands. The red was warm and inviting. She was reminded of embers in the fire during the coldest months of the year. She was reminded of hot soup flowing down her throat. She was reminded of red, red lips.

Before the young woman could prevent herself, her hands opened the bottle and she brought it to her mouth. It was only a sip. The smallest measurement of liquid ran past her lips, but it was enough. She could feel her blood cells charge and heat up her skin. For a moment, she felt as though she was on fire. Yet this revelation did not disturb her. In fact, she felt... weightless. As though all of her troubles had ceased to be.

The young woman had consumed alcohol before. She had even been intoxi -cated before. This was different. She had never felt this way before in her life.

"Scullery maid?" Came a voice, one which shocked the young woman back into her own skin. "Scullery maid!"

She recognized the voice's owner to be that of the queen's. She shoved the bottle into the pocket of her apron and ran upstairs in the kitchen. She took a deep, long bow as she enter, "forgive me, my queen, I was..."

What explanation could she give? She was certain her disobedience was written across her face as her cheeks flushed red. In her fortune, the queen interrupted.

"I have no time for your excuses. Since this staff's level of incompetence is nothing short of unspeakable, I am here myself to deliver my husband's order of white wine."

'Oh, then the other problem was solved', thought the young woman. She looked up as crates were carried in. That was when her eyes caught sight of the queen herself.

She had of course seen the queen prior to this night. However, something about her perspective had shifted. The queen's hair looked especially fine. It wafted over her shoulders in the most perfect shape, and it shone even in the kitchen's dim light. Her eyes were half-lidded, decorated diamonds which flickered as she turned her head. Then there were her lips. The deep, red shade, exactly the same as the wine which had been secretly collected.

The young woman felt as though she had started to float. Suddenly, she could see a life between her and the queen. She saw the two of them waking up together, having breakfast, planning out their day, going for walks. There was nothing else in this world she wanted more than to be near her queen. It was elation, it was freedom. It was love.

The young woman was in love with her queen. The beautiful and powerful queen. The one who demanded respect from her subjects and who deserved it. The one who deserved the very best meals of the world because she was simply the greatest queen in the world.

The wine was delivered, and as quickly as the queen had come in, she had vanished. Now it was simply the young woman, alone in the kitchen once more. But she didn't mind. She finally had a purpose in life. And that was to make the most eloquent food for her queen. She set straight to work.

The young woman had never moved so fast and diligently in her life. She sliced the vegetables thin and clean. She simmered her sauces to perfection. And the meat she cooked was so tender, it fell apart at the lightest squeeze.

Then she prepared the wine and set it on the trays for delivery. She didn't know what she was expecting — praise, perhaps? The recognition of a job well done by her favorite person? Just being in the presence of her queen was enough, she decided.

She entered the royal dining hall. The plates were set before the queen and king. Then the meal was laid out before them. The young woman watched with great anticipation as the queen drew up her first forkful of food.

The queen nodded in approval. "This is delicious. I'm not sure what it is that's different, but it tastes like..."

'It was made with love,' the young woman wanted to profess.

The king also shared his compliments, but the young woman hardly noticed. She had eyes only for her queen. Yet as she witnessed the rulers take another bite, she felt a sudden... hunger.

Not for the attention she had been craving only moments ago, but rather, for her own dinner. She had been the one who spent hours in the kitchen cooking, while the king and queen only sat there in wait. This delicious meal should be hers, but instead she would receive only scraps.

She looked at the queen again, and wondered how she had let herself become so infatuated. She had truly believed that she was in love with this woman. This greedy, selfish woman who did nothing but take from others. What had just happened?

The young woman put a hand to her lips and ran her fingers over them. The wine. That was when the sensations had started, and they had only been exacerbated when she laid eyes on the queen. There was only one conclusion — she must have drunk a love potion.

The young woman suddenly felt extremely uncomfortable. As though she had been a part of something awful against her will. She wanted to erase the memories of everything that had just happened. Except, nothing had actually happened. She merely did her job, albeit with more enthusiasm than usual.

The young woman began to feel a new sensation. She felt as though every-thing inside of her was crashing. There was an overwhelming sense of drowsiness washing over her. Her head pounded against her skull, as though her brain was trying to break through to find refuge. She feared that she may pass out.

Then the meal ended, and she was left alone to collect the dishes. Even though she had been cooking for hours without any rest. Even though she was feeling utterly broken, she was still left with work to do.

The young woman inhaled deeply and set about her job. As she made her way back to the kitchen, she tripped on her own feet and the dishes went soaring out of her hands. The young woman knew she had to pick them up before the king and queen saw, but instead she just laid there and cried. Oh, what an evening! How could things have gone so wrong?

Then she started to recall how she felt when she had taken her sip from the love potion. Nothing about her situation had changed, she had only felt better about it. She hadn't minded all of the work because her head had been so clouded by her heart. Even if the feelings weren't real, they had still been nice.

She thought about what would happen if she took another sip. Would all of this pain go away? Would she once more feel as though she were floating, and longed for nothing except to please her queen? It certainly seemed like a better alternative than the situation she currently found herself in.

The young woman reached for the bottle still stashed away in her apron. The glass felt cool against her skin. The liquid had retained its ruby-red glow. Once more, the young woman felt a warmth overcome her. Even before she managed to place it against her lips to drink from, the young woman had opened her mouth. The instant it touched her tongue, she felt her headache dissipate.

"What are you doing?" A voice from behind her demanded. The young woman felt herself become ecstatic as she recognized it as the voice of her beloved. "What is this mess? Clean it up at once, or I'll have your head removed!"

The young woman only nodded at her words. They were such beautiful words coming from her. She got up and did as instructed. All the while, she felt as though she were floating on air. How could she possibly feel so gloomy when someone as beautiful and magnificent as the queen was nearby?

The rest of the night went on like a dream, until the young woman finally headed to bed herself. In her mind, she saw images of her queen play out. She dreamt of all the wonderful foods she could cook for her majesty, and how everyday she could bring her queen a little bit of happiness. That was enough. It had to be enough.

When the sun rose the next morning, the young woman found herself unable to get out of bed. The sun shone far more brightly than it ever had before, and it burned her eyes. She wanted to roll over and never leave from her covers. She felt simultaneously too warm and too cold. The thought of getting up for another day of hard labor was too much to bear.

Yet what choice did she have? Staying in bed was not an option, as deeply as she wished it. The king and queen needed to be fed, and she was their cook. As she arose, the bottle from last night fell from her pillow. To her great relief, it had not shattered upon hitting the ground. However, this did not calm the young woman as she acknowledged its presence. She must have forgotten that she had brought it to her room. Once more, she picked it up and inspected its contents. And once more, she was tempted to drink from it.

She thought of the risks. She couldn't keep this up forever, after all. What if anyone found out? Would it cost her this job, her life?

It was more than that, however. She didn't like that the feelings she developed were against her will. All the same, did she help herself by remaining broken and helpless? The young woman fell to the ground, unable to hold up her own weight any longer. She knew it was wrong, and yet she didn't care. If one little sip was all it took for her to get through the day, then what did it matter to anyone else? There was plenty in the bottle, she could make this last for months. Years.

She just had to work.

So she drank, and immediately stepped up to start her day. Just like before, the weight of the world had been lifted. She felt nothing but energetic as she worked for her beautiful queen. Back and forth this little game played.

The young woman hated herself every time she took a drink from the bottle, and yet she did nothing to stop herself. Soon, a single sip wasn't enough. She found the effects wore off much quicker than before, and she had to consume more. Suddenly, she was taking whole gulps throughout the day.

It wasn't long afterwards that the bottle became empty.

The young woman wailed as she felt the effects leave her and the aftermath settle in. She cried for her body, which felt broken and torn. She wanted out of this cycle, and yet she did not know how to stop. Especially when she knew where to find more.

That evening, before preparing the royal dinner, the young woman went back to the wine cellar. She opened the secret compartment and entered it. What she witnessed down there was a horrifying sight. The chamber had been emptied.

The young woman fell to her knees and wept bitterly. What was she to do now? Where had the supply gone?

"I had it moved," a voice said.

The same voice which always seemed to be interrupting her thoughts. The young woman turned up to see the queen waiting for her. Yet something was different about her. The usual aura of authority was depleted. Were it not for the fancy dress and jewelry, the young woman would have mistaken the queen for anyone else in the kingdom.

"You need to leave," the queen went on. "It's not... safe here. Not now that you know this secret."

The young woman got up on her feet. "Why?"

The queen did not say anything. She just smiled. It was the saddest expression the young woman had ever seen. She didn't know why it had never crossed her mind before. Why was there a chamber full of love potion to begin with? There was only one reason, of course, and she stood there.

Two women, both broken.

"Come with me," the young woman persisted.

She had felt hours of love for this queen. Even if they were false, she couldn't deny them. Especially now that she saw the queen as she truly was. She wondered what kind of ruler she would have been had she not entered this cycle. The young woman also wondered how cruel the king must be to his own wife to make her choose this.

The queen shook her head. "I never had a choice in the matter. This is my life."

The young woman understood. "In that case, let me prepare one last dinner for you."

The two headed back up to the kitchen, and the queen watched on as the young woman cooked. Her head still ached, but the pain was starting to die down. She worked until the meal was prepared. Then the two of them went to the dining hall where the king was waiting.

The queen took her seat next to him. When she was handed her wine, she took a long drink.

THE OLD WOMAN AND THE MERMAID

Once upon a time, there was an old woman. She lived on an island. It was vastly covered by the widespread of the ocean, which meant she had no way of getting out. It also meant that very few people knew where to find her. It had been many years since she had last seen another person. But she did not mind. She chose to stay on this island, even if it meant that she was all alone.

The old woman felt that she could not leave, for many years ago, when she was much younger, she had a child. The two of them lived on this island together, and they were happy. But her child had been very small, and had not yet learned the dangers of the ocean.

One morning, the child had crawled out of bed before their mother had awoken, and went to the shoreline. They entered the ocean, and never came back out. By the time the woman had seen what had happened, it was too late. She found her child's remains and buried them beneath her house.

And so, she could not leave this island, because it would mean that her child would be left here without anyone.

One day, as the old woman was preparing her morning tea, a storm had set in. It did not fall from the sky like rain, but rather, it came up from the sea. Its waters rose until it lapped at the foot of her house. Soon, the water was seeping in from the walls and filled up the rooms. The old woman was walking around waist-deep in sea water. Yet she did not stop her routine.

The waters were cold and gave her a rash, but she did not stop her routine.

The critters of the sea made their way into her house next. They planted themselves against her wooden walls and swam about her rooms, but she did not stop her routine.

The foundation of her house creaked and screamed in protest, begging for the water to go down or it would break, break, break. But she did not stop her routine. You see, she had lived this way for so long, that she did not know what else to do.

It was only when a new noise made itself known that her curiosity had been piqued. It was a sound she had not heard in decades, apart from her own. It was the sound of someone crying. The old woman looked out of her window and saw a mermaid. She was perched up on a rock out past the shoreline. Her voice rang above the waters and over to the old woman's house.

It was not a simple cry, as though she had just like her favorite pearl or sea shell. It was a deep, wailing cry. The old woman knew the sound well. The mermaid's heart had been broken.

The old woman made her way out of her house. It had been a long time since she had last gone for a swim, yet her muscles remembered what to do. Slowly but surely she reached the mermaid.

At first, the aquatic creature took no notice of her. She continued to cry her broken song as though she was still the only one there. The old woman knew that feeling, as well.

The mermaid was staring at one spot in particular on the island, the same way the old woman had once stared into the ocean where she had found the body of her child. This mermaid must have had a child as well, and it had been beached. In an attempt to save them, the mermaid had conjured up this storm. But it must have been too late.

The old woman swam out to where the mermaid had been staring at, and her suspicions were confirmed. There was indeed the remains of a much smaller mermaid. She wrapped them up, gentle in a way only a mother who had lost a child could, and brought them to the mermaid.

She stared at the old woman in disbelief, before taking the remains from her grasp. As she held onto her child, the old woman wrapped her arms around the mermaid, and they both wept.

When they had finished, the mermaid let down the storm. The waters retreated back into the ocean. The old woman buried the mermaid's child next to her own. From then on, the mermaid visited the island everyday, and the two of them were finally no longer alone.

THE QUEEN AND THE FAIRY

Once upon a time, there was a queen. She lived in a beautiful castle. Her kingdom was considered the most prosperous in the land, and everyone loved her beauty and gentle nature. The queen should have been happy, but she wasn't. For her husband, the king, was not a kind man.

He would appear before his subjects with smiles and charm, so that they thought he was a good person. But when the doors were closed, he was very different to his wife. This made her afraid of him, yet she had no one to tell. Who in the kingdom would believe that her husband was truly a monster?

Everyday, she walked around the castle, trying to avoid the king at all costs. And every night, she knew she would have to return to him in their bed chamber. Then every morning, she woke up and hoped that something would change.

One day, the queen set out to the royal garden. She wanted to inspect how the flowers were growing. Flowers always brought her such happiness, for they were beautiful and fragile just like her. As she was peering around, she spotted a small yet potent light. It was a fairy!

The queen approached the little creature, slowly, because she did not want to frighten her away. The fairy, in turn, became curious about the queen. She had never met a human before, let alone a royal one. She had flown into the garden to sip on the morning dew, but now that she was caught, she felt it would be impolite to simply leave her host. This was the queen's garden, after all.

The fairy gave a deep curtsy, and this made the queen giggle. When it became apparent that the fairy was not going to fly away in fright, the queen held out her palm. The fairy accepted the invitation, and took a seat within her hand. Then the two of them walked back up to the castle.

The fairy was enchanted by the scenery. She had only ever seen the castle from the outside before, and she had always wondered what was inside. She looked with great interest at the candles, tapestries, stained-glass windows and servants. There were so many people, it was no wonder why this place had to be so big!

The queen was pleased to share her world with another, especially one so enthusiastic. Her mood dropped dramatically when her husband, the king, walked by. She shut her hands tight over the fairy so he would not see. For he would surely make her discard the fairy the same way he had gotten rid of all the good things in her life.

To her relief, he merely greeted her, then left to attend other duties. Once he was gone, she opened her palms to inspect her new friend. She was horrified to discover that she had hurt her fairy. The little creature was wincing in her grasp. The queen did her best to smooth out her wings. She needed to help the fairy. She needed to keep her safe, so that something like this would never happen again.

She took her friend into a spare room where her husband never visited. It had a big, beautiful window and lots of places for the fairy to play in. She should be perfectly happy here. And at first, the fairy was.

She flew around from shelf to shelf on the wall, pushing over books to open them. She would ask the queen questions about the pictures she saw inside. The two of them would spend hours inside that room, talking about everything and nothing. They would sit by the window and stare out into the world. The queen would often wonder what it would be like to run away from all of this. To take her new friend and leave everything behind.

In those moments, she felt that she was truly happy.

Except, one detail started to bother her. Whenever they stared at the window, she noticed her fairy would look a little too fondly at the sky and the birds flying past them. She would run to the edge of the window, as though she was preparing to join them. The queen did not want this. She did not want her friend to leave her all alone.

Then on a day when the birds were especially close and cheerful, the fairy did indeed begin to fly out of the window. In a panic, the queen grabbed for her. She reached for one of her wings and tore it off. She placed the fairy back down on the windowsill, but the fairy lost balance and fell over. She was not used to standing with a torn wing.

The queen petted her hair, and brought the fairy fresh flowers to cheer her up. Yet she remained unhappy. The queen did other things to make up for what she had done. She brought her fairy toys and jewelry. She read her stories and sang her songs. Yet nothing the queen did seemed to cheer up the little fairy.

As the days went on, the fairy played with her less and less. She seemed to always be staring out into the sky, dreaming. The queen missed what they used to have, and she became determined to get those good days back. She just needed a little more time. She needed the fairy to be patient with her.

Then the next day, the queen caught the fairy trying to climb down from the window. She quickly scooped up her little friend and placed her inside of a golden birdcage. Now she would not have to worry about being alone anymore.

As for the fairy, she would sit in that cage and cry for hours and hours. She missed her family, and her freedom. She would have come back to visit the queen, if she had been given the choice to. Now, however, the fairy only wanted to leave this place.

To pass the time, the fairy often watched the birds. She envied them. She longed to join them. Then once, when she was feeling especially lonely, the fairy began to sing out to the birds. Her voice was soft, and she worried they would not hear it, but she was too tired to sing any louder.

To her surprise, however, the birds responded. She sang her song, and they returned it. She continued to sing, and they continued to echo. Eventually, the birds came over to where her cage had been placed. She reached out and petted them. She enjoyed the soft texture of their feathers.

They repeated the song, but it was much louder in the room, and she became afraid. She worried that if the queen came back, she would force the birds out. Just as she had taken everything else from the fairy.

She tried to shoo the birds away herself, as a warning, but they did not listen. She tried to wave her arms frantically to make them understand how dire the situation was, but they did not listen. Finally, the fairy slapped the birds. This time, they did leave.

The fairy fell to her knees and cried. She wanted to apologize. She wanted to tell the birds that she hadn't meant to, that she was only trying to keep them safe. But it was too late, and she knew that they would never return.

As she sat in the cage and cried, she could hear footsteps approaching her room. She knew that the queen would come in soon enough. The fairy decided right then and there that she could not tolerate one more day of this life. She slammed all of her strength into the side of the cage.

At first, nothing happened, but soon enough, the cage started to move. She continued to use the last of her energy to push it forward. She heard the door open, and the queen gasp, but the fairy did not stop. The cage fell forward just as the queen was about to grab for it.

The fairy felt herself falling, falling, falling.

The fairy had never fallen before. She supposed she had better get used to it. She would never fly again, after all.

The cage hit the ground and smashed into pieces. The fairy was in immense pain, but she was free, at last. It took a long time before she mustered the strength to be able to sit up. By then, the sun was beginning to set. The fairy took one last look at the castle, at the window which had been her prison. She could see the queen alone in her room, watching her, yet not moving. The fairy turned her back and walked away.

As she stepped into the forest, a noise caught her attention. She traveled in deeper until she came across a unicorn. It was a magnificent creature, pure and wonderful, but it was caught in a trap. The fairy looked up it with great pity in her heart. She had to help it. She had to keep it safe. She had to keep it hidden, so nothing like this could ever happen again.

THE HARPY AND THE NAGA

Once upon a time, there was a harpy. She lived alone, deep in the woods. The only time she came out was at night to hunt. She preferred not to be seen, if it could be helped. For she was the last of her kind.

There was a time many centuries ago, when the harpy was part of a powerful flock. She was surrounded by her sisters, and they were all fierce warriors. Men would tremble at their might. Until a time came when humans were able to invent weapons strong enough to strike down the harpies. One by one, her sisters fell.

Now she was alone and too afraid to come out into the light.

One night, the harpy set off for her hunt only to discover that she could not find any game. She traveled far and wide across the forest in search of food, yet none could be found. The harpy landed herself on a nearby branch, confused and a little concern. If she could not find anything to eat, she would have to go into the village and take from the humans. Her mouth salivated at the thought of cattle, but she shook it away when she realized she had to determine what had happened to her prey.

Perhaps there was a disease which had wiped them out? But no, even a virus would not work so quickly. Besides, she would have felt the impacts. Then maybe her prey ran out of food? Except the forest was lush. There was only one conclusion, then — another predator had moved into her territory. The harpy felt something which she hadn't in a very long time. She felt a twinge of hope. Was the new predator in her forest a harpy? Was she not truly the last? Despite her hunger, the harpy felt a renewed sense of energy and soared into the night.

She searched high into the trees. When no harpy made themselves known, she began to call out. Her voice rang across the trees, but still no harpy came. So, she dipped down lower, below the top of the trees and back into the forest. Her eyes scanned around as she had for her hunt, but still no other harpy appeared.

Then, finally, she saw something. It was a long trail of blood. It stained the ground of the forest. She recognized the smell of deer. Whatever had come into her woods was nearby. The harpy felt herself becoming afraid. If this creature was not like her, and she suspecting it wasn't, then what was brave enough to come into her territory?

She flew in deeper and deeper, following the trail of blood, until she came across a grotto. Within its shallow pool, was a naga. The creature was in the middle of her meal. Her jaw was unhinged so that she could swallow her prey whole. The harpy hid back behind the trees. She had never seen such a sight. What was she to do? A creature that powerful would not be so easily taken down. The harpy wished that she was not alone, that her sisters were here to help her in this endeavor. The disappointment that she was indeed the last of her kind had been enough to break her heart.

Despite herself, the harpy began to weep. In her sorrow, she did not notice the shadow which was approaching her, until a voice spoke. It was slow and ancient, as though it had been many centuries since this voice had last been used.

"Why... are you... crying?"

The harpy looked up and gazed into the eyes of the naga. She could see her scaly skin. She could smell the blood and death on the naga's tongue. The harpy flew up into the trees.

"Wait...! Come... back!" cried the naga. "I didn't... mean... to frighten you... I have never... met...someone... like me..."

Someone like her? This confused the harpy. She and the naga could not be more different. She was covered in feathers and flew around the sky. The naga was scaly and crawled around the ground. The harpy had once been part of a flock, and while she had never met a naga in person before, she knew from stories that they were solitary creatures.

She thought that these words must have been a trick. The naga could not fly, and therefore was trying to lure the harpy back down to devour her. Still, what a strange thing to say in order to coax prey.

But then she thought about it — when had been the last time the harpy had spoken to another monster? All the animals in the forest were just that. Animals. They did not have the power of speech the way man and monsters did. Which meant it had been many years since the harpy had last spoken herself. She landed on a branch, close enough to talk to the naga, but far away enough to escape quickly.

Her own voice cracked as she asked, "who... are you...?"

The naga smiled. "I come... from a land... far away. I... have traveled... the world... many times... in search of food. It has been... a long time... since I have come... to this forest... but now... I am back..."

The harpy tried to think back to when she had her flock, if she had seen this naga once before. Nothing came to mind, so it must have been very long ago indeed. Back when she still had her sisters to keep her company.

"And you are... here... to feed...?" the harpy asked, to which the naga nodded. "But this is... my home... I have... never left... what will... I eat...?"

The naga smiled again. "I will have... eaten my fill...soon. I do not... need to eat... for very long... but I can go... decades... in between... meals. Perhaps... we could... share...?"

The harpy thought about it for a moment. She had nothing to gain from sharing with the naga. She could insist that this was her home and that the naga needed to leave. But she thought about what it would be like to speak to someone again. To share stories again.

"How long... will you... need to feed...?" she asked.

"Give me... one year..." the naga answered. "And then... I will be... on my way."

A year was not so long to beings as ancient as they were. The harpy saw no harm in allowing the naga permission into her forest for that time. Then, if the year ran up and the naga was still present, then she would insist upon her departure. And so, the compromise was made.

By the next night, some of the prey had moved back into the forest, and the two of them set out for a hunt once more. The harpy soared into the air, and caught unsuspecting prey from the sky. The naga remained low to the ground, and would strike her meals from the back.

As the two sat down to eat, they would talk to each other. The harpy would share stories about her sisters. How they ruled the skies together, and the humans used to fear their might. The naga would talk about all the different lands she had seen. She would describe the many different humans and animals. She would describe the different climates, and plants which grew.

It sounded like a wondrous, yet lonely life. But the naga said she did not mind, that it was the way of her people to be solitary.

"Have you... ever met... another naga...?" the harpy asked.

"Once..." she replied. "I had... children... many, many years ago... I watched them hatch... and then I left..."

That sounded dreadfully sad to the harpy, who had raised many of her own children. "Do you... miss them...?"

The naga shook her head. "They are... out in the world... and that... is enough for me."

"How do you... manage... to never... be around... your own kind...?"

"I am... now..."

The naga had a very strange way of viewing the world, at least to the harpy. But she would admit, she did enjoy their talks together. It very quickly became her favorite part of the day. She would rush through the hunt just so they could sit together and converse.

The naga, in turn, also had a world of patience for the harpy. She would listen and nod as she told her story after story about her kin. What a sad existence — to miss your family.

When the winter months came, things were more difficult. The naga could not move so easily, and often the harpy had to wrap her wings around her. That was the only time the naga would allow herself to be held. The harpy adored pressing their bodies against one another. She even found that she no longer minded the texture of the naga's scales against her feathers.

When spring came, those times stopped, and the harpy felt sorrow. Not just for the lack of intimacy, but also because she realized that their time together was growing short. This caused her great pain, for she had fallen in love with the naga.

Before she knew it, the day had come at last. The harpy waited until nightfall before joining her naga. She tried to smile as her friend made her presence known.

"It is time..." the naga stated. "After tonight... I will... no longer... haunt your forest..."

"Is that... all you... think we are...?"

"Is it... not true...?"

The harpy shook her head. She wanted to share her feelings with her naga, but she knew that they would not be understood. Not because the naga wouldn't want to understand — she saw the two of them as equals. It was simply her nature. The harpy would not begrudge her for it. She was in love with her, after all.

So instead, she asked, "will you... ever... return...?"

"If you... will have me... I need... to move... to feed... if you will... permit me... then I shall... return in time..."

The harpy smiled. After many years of being alone, she had learned to be patient. She could wait as long as she knew that her naga would return. Then the two of them set out for their hunt, one last time. They feasted and conversed one last time. Then they sat in silence, one last time. Sleep betrayed the harpy as her eyes closed. When she woke up the next morning, her naga had already left.

Then the harpy flew back to her treetops and prepared for her long wait. She found that, despite being alone, knowing her friend was out there, made her feel less lonely.

THE FISHERMAN'S WIFE AND THE SELKIE

Once upon a time, there was a fisherman. He had a wife. She was a quiet and timid woman who stayed in their little cottage all day long. While he was out at sea, she made sure their home stayed clean, both inside and out. She prepared all the meals so he would have a lovely dinner to come home to. She made sure that their children were fed and bathed. Then she would wash the sheets for their bed.

They both told themselves that they were happy.

One day, the fisherman went out into a fog. His wife stood from the window and watched until his boat disappeared. She sighed deeply, and secretly, she wished that he would not return. But that was a horrible thing to think. He was a good man, or at least, he used to be.

He always brought home fish from his trips, which kept them fed and a roof over their heads. He was good with the children. She told herself that this was enough. It was just that... sometimes, when it was late and the children were already asleep, she and her husband would sit by the fireplace in silence. She would look over at him and see a longing in his eyes reflected in the flames. She recognized the look because she often wore it herself.

They told themselves they were happy.

Their house was atop a hill overlooking the ocean, and the fisherman's wife would often walk out there and listen to the waves. The sound of the sea was like music for her soul. It was the only thing which brought any comfort in her life. Its song would uplift her before she headed back inside that cottage and into her small world.

She often wondered what it would be like if she and her husband switched places. If she was the one who went out to sea every day, and he stayed home with the children. Would they find solace in that?

The fog had lifted before dinner that evening, and the fisherman's wife could see her husband pull into the docks. She used to wait for him down there. Those were the days when he would rush back home to her. But now, she simply waited in the kitchen. Better to make sure that his dinner was kept hot.

As he entered the cottage, his wife discovered that he was not alone. There was a woman in his grasp. A frightened woman, with big dark eyes. The type of eyes which told a story and showed the whole soul within them. The kind of eyes which broke a person's heart.

The fisherman's wife could tell from her vacant expression, wet hair, and the leather pelt wrapped around her that this woman was a selkie. She must have swam up to her husband, curious and carefree. He recognized what she was, and captured her.

"She will be staying here with us from now on," the fisherman explained with a smile.

His wife did not protest. She wanted to tell him that this was a foolish idea, that they should set this poor creature free, but she did not say a word. She had never defied her husband before. She had never defied anyone before, actually, even as a young girl. She had always been told that her obedience was her most prized asset.

Such a prize, that this was where it brought her — a little house, full of children, and now home to her husband's captured selkie.

The first few days were an adjustment. The creature... or rather, the woman... the fisherman's wife really wasn't sure what to call her... was slow in her movements. She did not speak as she wandered up and down the little house, inspecting all of the silverware and pottery as though they were a lost language. She stared at the children as though they were foreign to her, as well. They didn't seem to mind, however, they were too young to understand.

She seemed consumed with all things shiny. She would hold up spoons to the window and watch for hours as the sunlight reflected off of them. The fisherman's wife found herself almost envious — imagine living a life where the simplicity of a spoon's reflection could bring such fascination.

She thinks this is what her husband sees in the selkie. That she is a shiny, new object that he wants to glisten in the window for hours, even though he was not home. He knew that the selkie waited for him in his house, and to him, that was enough.

After a week, the fisherman's wife took the selkie out around back to help with the laundry. The selkie was captivated by the bubbles the soap produced, and the fisherman's wife wondered if it reminded her of sea foam. For the first time since her arrival, she smiled. Then the fisherman's wife smiled, too.

When the chores were finished and there was still time enough before her husband's return, the fisherman's wife stood outside of her house to listen to her sea's song. She danced alongside the waves as the lullaby soothed her soul once again. Only this time, she realized that she was not standing out there alone.

She turned to see the selkie, standing there, watching her. No judgment on her face. Just those dark, heartbreak eyes. Soon, she stepped closer to the fisherman's wife, and began a dance of her own. Like of all her movements, it was slow and calculated, but graceful and delicate. The sort of movement which only comes from a creature who had lived a lifetime in the sea. The fisherman's wife found that she could not take her eyes off of the sight. Then for a moment, she felt something she hadn't in years. She felt truly happy.

"Where is my dinner?" Came her husband's voice.

The two stopped their dancing to look back at the little cottage. It was then that the fisherman's wife realized how low the sun had set. She had never lost track of time like that before.

There in the doorway stood her husband, his face turned down in a scowl as he looked at her. But when his eyes shifted over to the selkie, he smiled. His wife could not decide which face was more frightening. All the same, the two of them returned to the house, and the fisherman's wife began to cook dinner.

After that evening, she became much more careful around the selkie. She did not think the creature was dangerous, but she acknowledged that she didn't fully understand her, either. She was a being as mysterious as the sea, and she belonged in such a place.

The fisherman's wife still found herself staring out into the ocean and wonderd if she belonged to such a place, as well. She sometimes wondered if that had been her reason for marrying her husband in the first place — because she knew it would bring her closer to the sea. She had never known what she had wanted from life except to be close to the ocean. She wondered if that was how the selkie felt now that she was trapped in this house.

It wasn't fair. Her husband should have known better than to do this to a creature who had no business being kept like a pet. The fisherman's wife decided right then and there that she would search around the house for the selkie's pelt. It wouldn't be difficult, considering her husband spent the day away on his boat, and expected to come home to a clean house. If he asked where the selkie went, she would simple say that the creature had discovered her own pelt and made her escape. Who would he be to question this?

And so, the fisherman's wife began her search. She looked high up on the roof, and down below in their cellar. She looked within their tool shed, and out in the garden. She searched every room in their little cottage. She turned up the floorboards and every hidden corner — yet she found nothing.

The fisherman's wife sat down and thought about where her husband could have possibly hidden the pelt. But the answer came over her all too quickly. Of course, where else would he keep it, but in his boat, far away from them all day long. Feeling discouraged, his wife began to cry.

She couldn't remember the last time she had cried. She supposed it must have been around the time the children were born. She was not miserable with her family. She just wasn't happy either. She was only happy when she was dancing out by the sea, with the selkie.

That was when she realized that she did not want the selkie to leave. The creature had given her something her family never seemed to. She had given the fisherman's wife company. Without her, no matter how many children they surrounded themselves with, the fisherman's wife would always feel alone.

There was a little sound, and she saw that she was no longer alone in the room. The fisherman's wife turned up to see the selkie standing at the doorway. The creature walked over and took a seat next to her. She still spook no words, but there was something in the look she gave which made the fisherman's wife understand what they needed to do.

That night, when her husband came home, the house was clean and his dinner was hot. He frowned at his wife and smiled at the selkie. When his wife put the children to bed, he took the selkie to their bedroom. While they were in there, his wife strode down to the docks, where he had tied up his boat. She rummaged through his things, but it did not take long for her to discover the leather pelt admist his fishing supplies.

She was quiet as she entered the house once more, and even more quiet as she opened the door to their bedroom. She did not want to wake up her husband. The moonlight glinted through the window as she stepped inside. Its glow revealed the selkie as she sat up in bed, staring down at the man who had kidnapped her.

The fisherman's wife joined her in looking at him. He had not been a good husband, but he was a good father. She had been a good wife, but perhaps not a good mother. And maybe this was the way things were supposed to be. She could not break something which had already been broken.

She handed over the leather pelt to the selkie, who took it and ran. The fisherman's wife sprinted after her, no longer caring if they were making noise. It didn't matter now.

The two of them continued to run until they were out of the house, down the hill, and at the shoreline. The selkie walked into the ocean until it was up to her knees, and then she began to pull the pelt over her head. Her temporary pause gave the fisherman's wife a moment to catch up. She climbed into her husband's boat as the transformation concluded, and where once stood a woman was now a seal. The fisherman's wife chased after her, until the sun began to peak up and she realized that she could no longer see her house.

This was real. It was truly happening. She was leaving her life behind.

At that moment, the selkie jumped onto the boat. The sudden movement startled the fisherman's wife, but as she looked over at the creature, she saw the same look in her eyes as she had before. The one which was full of understanding and empathy. The one which told the fisherman's wife that she was free at last.

Then the two of them headed out further into the sea.

THE MERMAID AND THE SELKIE

Once upon a time, there was a mermaid and a selkie. They had known each other all their lives, and were the closest of friends. When they had first met, the mermaid had a fish tail and a human torso, but the selkie resembled only a seal. Mermaids had a way of knowing other magical creatures, however, so they recognized one another.

They would play for hours and hours, passing their immortal lives together. As they grew, soon came the time for them to walk among the humans. Mermaids and selkies could only go up at night, and only after they came of age. The mermaid was excited, and also a little nervous. She would not change so significantly, she would merely trade in her tail for legs. But she had only known her selkie friend as a seal. She wondered what she would look like when they went above the shore.

The two of them received their family's blessings as they traveled up the waters and onto the nearby beach. As the mermaid left the ocean and her scales dried up, her tail split in two and she found herself with a pair of legs. Then she turned to watch her friend transform.

The selkie took much longer than the mermaid. She drew from her body, as though her leather pelt was only a coat to be removed. Slowly but surely, a young woman pulled out. The mermaid gasped as her friend took her first steps. She was a lovely sight to behold.

The mermaid soon rose up herself, and the two walked hand in hand into the town. They did not notice the strange looks everyone gave them, they only saw the wonders of the upper world. They saw the plants and animals, they saw the buildings and the automobiles. They saw sparkling jewelry, which the selkie especially liked. They saw the art all around them, on the walls and on the windows. They could smell the food and hear the music.

It was truly a wonder to behold. But, it was not quite as wondrous, the mermaid thought, as seeing her friend like this for the first time.

She wondered what life would be like for them after this day. When they returned to the waters, and the mermaid saw her selkie friend as only a seal once again, she would forever think of the girl lost inside. She would remember her beautiful eyes and her soft hair. She would remember her lovely voice when she laughed. The mermaid had not realized she could feel this way about another person before.

The night went by too quickly as the sun began to rise. The two of them wished to sit on the beach and watch as it ascended, but they knew that there were risks to being out once night ended. She wondered if the two of them would ever return to land, even though she knew the consequences of that. If a mermaid left the sea too often, her tail would remain as legs permanently. But selkies needed to leave the water every so often once they came of age. Or they would forget they were magical creatures and become seals forever.

The two of them made their way back to the sea. The mermaid simply had to step inside the waters for her tail to reappear, but the selkie again took much longer. She pulled her leather pelt over her head and the transformation began to take place. The mermaid watched as her friend resumed her usual form.

Once they were both home, their families asked them about the trip. The mermaid was asked what she saw on land, but she found that she could not recall anything specific. She only remembered the selkie's beautiful face.

The next day started off typical enough for the pair. They woke up, ate breakfast and began their games. The mermaid was having fun, but there was something different in the way she felt. She and her selkie friend were playing as they always had when they were children, but the mermaid found that she still could not stop thinking about the beautiful woman who was underneath the leather pelt.

The mermaid wondered if she might sneak away once in a while when her friend went above sea. It surely could not hurt to do so for just a short while. Especially if it meant that she could walk hand in hand with her lovely friend again.

The next time the selkie needed to leave the waters, the mermaid did exactly that. Her friend was more than willing to keep the secret. Sure enough, as the two left the shallows, the mermaid found herself with two legs, and waited until her friend stood up to join her. She was even lovelier than the mermaid had remembered. They took one another's hand and walked into town.

Once again, they did not mind the looks they received from the humans around them. The selkie had eyes for everything, and the mermaid had eyes only for her friend. And the mermaid felt that this was the happiest she had ever been in her life. So much so, that when the sun began to rise, she could feel her heart break.

If only there was a way to have more time...

"Let us stay," she told her friend before they were able to step into the ocean's waters once more. "We can watch the sunrise and go back in the morning."

The selkie was hesitant, but in the end, she agreed. They did indeed watch the sun come up, and it was a lovely time. As the morning shifted into day, however, the mermaid found herself looking less at the sky and more at her friend. She was by far the beautiful sight to behold, and the mermaid did not want to miss a second of it.

There was a twisting inside where her heart was, a mixture of anguish and serenity. She was happy to be at the selkie's side, but a part of her felt as though it would never be the same again. All she wanted was to lie here forever, but the reality was that she could not, and this thought broke her heart.

Yes, that was it. Her heart was broken, for she was in love with her friend.

Soon, the selkie fell asleep, and the mermaid had an idea. She picked up her friend's leather pelt, and ran into town. She hid it in a place she would not forget, but where no one would look. Then, she returned to the beach and slept.

At nightfall, the mermaid was awoken by sobbing. She sat up to see that her friend was crying. When she asked what was wrong, the selkie stammered on about her missing pelt.

"Oh..." the mermaid replied, suddenly feeling guilty. She didn't know what she had been thinking, but it somehow hadn't crossed her mind how the decision would impact her friend's feelings. She had just wanted a little more time. "We... we shall go and look for it together. It must have been humans, that's the only explanation."

The selkie nodded, but tears still fell from her eyes. "We must hurry, for your sake, too."

"Pardon?"

"If we don't return to the sea soon, you'll also be trapped inside this human body forever."

Trapped. That had been the word she used. Did she really feel as though these forms were the enemy? The mermaid had felt that for the first time in their lives, she and her friend were on equal footing. Had she been mistaken? Did the selkie truly not feel the same way she did?

The mermaid felt her heartbreak all over again. Then she realized that there was no point in hiding the truth. She needed to say what was on her mind now, or risk losing her friend forever.

"What if..." she started. "That wasn't the worst thing?"

"What are you talking about?"

"I mean... what if we stayed as humans? Do we not have fun up here?"

The selkie shook her head. "It is not about that. The land is not our home."

"What if I want it to be my home?"

"Don't be silly! Why would you ever want that?"

"Because..." the mermaid took a step into the waters. The ocean pooled around her ankles, and yet they remained feet. "I means that I can stay here with you."

The selkie had no words. She stood there for a time, until tears ran down her cheeks. The mermaid ran to her side and wrapped her arms around her friend. The selkie went on.

"You should never have even come with me, it's dangerous. But I... I wanted you to come with me. We do everything together. I wanted you to see me as I am — the girl underneath the seal pelt."

At her words, the mermaid realized she had been wrong about the situation. This was all new to both of them, and so sudden. They had been friends their whole lives, and now... she didn't have the words to describe the way love had crept up on her. But going behind the selkie's back wasn't the answer.

Now it was too late. The sun had peaked up, and the mermaid would never be able to return to the sea again. She could not condemn her friend to the same fate. How were they going to make this work?

"What... what do we do now?" she asked.

The selkie smiled and offered her hand. "We take it one step at a time."

The two of them walked back into town, and the mermaid showed where she had hidden the leather pelt. Then they rushed back to the sea, but the selkie did not immediately transform. Instead, she looked back up at her friend.

"You know I will return to you?" She asked.

The mermaid nodded. "Yes, I do."

The selkie smiled. Then, while she had the time to, she leaned forward so the two of them could share a kiss. It was small and short, neither of them knew what to do. But it was a first kiss, and it was all theirs.

Then the mermaid watched as the selkie placed her pelt back over her body and rejoined the ocean in her seal form. She bobbed around in the shallows for a time, before disappearing beneath the waters. Now there was nothing left to do for the mermaid except to wait, until the love of her life returned.

In the meantime, she created a home of the island. She learned the language and made friends. There were struggles, but she managed to get by. Taking notice of her beauty, many men came to court her, but she always refused. Even when they offered her a life of comfort, she turned them down.

They never understood why. They came up with the theory that she once had a beloved, but he had died at sea. Why else would she wait by the shores, night after night, looking out as though she was waiting for someone to return?

THE SELKIE MOTHER

Once upon a time there was a selkie. She lived in the ocean with her three children, and they were happy. She taught them to be wary of the dangers within the world, such as predators. Leopard seals, sharks, but most importantly, she taught them to stay away from humans.

Her children did not understand this last one, as they knew that one day they would be able to walk among the land as humans themselves. But the selkie mother just shook her head. She did not want to tell the truth of how she became a mother in the first place.

She could still remember being young and curious as they were, longing for nothing more than to see the world above. How naive she had been, to think she was safe from humans just because she looked like one herself.

She feared for the day when her children came of age. In her desire to keep them safe, the selkie mother waited one night for her children to sleep, and then she swam up to the surface. She hopped onto the beaches, as she had so long ago, and stretched out her human body from under her leather pelt.

Soon enough, she was walking. She had only one goal to her mission — travel around the island, see what threats were out there, and then head back to her children. It was night, so most humans were asleep, but she knew that this did not mean the dangers were gone as well.

Without her leather pelt to keep her warm, the selkie mother found the cold air around her to be unbearable. She looked around for means of warmth, and in the distant woods, she could see smoke which she knew meant fire.

The selkie mother approached, and saw that the camp fire was lit by a single human. Getting closer, she could see that it was a woman. She felt a little more courageous in venturing forward, and stepped on a twig. At the sound of it breaking, the human woman stood up.

"Who goes there?" She bellowed out. She held a spear in her hand.

The selkie stopped, suddenly afraid. She was back at that place she had been the last time she was on the land. Her breathing became short and shallow, and the world began to spin.

The voice, which had spoken so harshly, now replied in a far softer tone. "Are you alright? Are you lost?"

Slowly, the selkie mother felt her breath slow down. The ground returned beneath her as she took a step forward.

"Who are you?" the woman asked. "What is your name?"

Despite her time on the land, she had not yet learned the language of humans. So as the woman asked her questions, the selkie mother could only give a pitiful stare. Eventually, the woman stopped asking so many questions and just offered her a seat by the fire. The selkie did not hesitant to sit and warm up.

The two sat in silence for a period. Then, the woman pulled out a bag, from which she produced a pair of fish. The selkie mother's mouth watered at the idea of cooking. That had been one of the few things she missed from the land. Humans possessed such creativity when it came to food. The woman placed her catch onto a stick and rotated it around the fire. The selkie mother watched as their meal bubbled and popped.

"You are strange to me," the woman went on, even though she knew the selkie mother did not understand. "I have lived on this island my entire life, and I've never seen anyone like you. I wonder where you come from?"

Even though the selkie mother did not know what specifically she was discussing, somehow she knew that the woman was suspecting her origins. There was an influx in a human's voice which she only heard in reference to herself. It made her pause, but the woman only smiled.

"It's alright," she continued. "The world would be far less interesting without people in it who were different. I never made much of a home on this island, I just... know nothing else..."

The selkie mother began to wonder where the woman's family was. She looked old enough to be a mother herself, surely she must have a husband or children. She had unloaded two fish, after all. Yet as the night waned on and the fish finished cooking, she realized that no other guests would be joining them. Which suited her just fine.

After her meal was over, the selkie mother felt that she had warmed sufficiently, and was ready to return home. She got up when she felt a tug at her arm.

"Wait!" the woman cried out.

The selkie mother had heard that word before, and she still remembered what it meant. She turned, and saw the most pitiful look she had ever seen on the woman's face. It tore at something deep inside of her, but it was not enough to keep her there. She had sleeping children to get back to, after all. At least now she knew that the human world had become kinder than the last time she had walked its lands.

She shook her head, a gesture which she understood, because it was one she had used before. She took her arm away from the woman's grasp, and there was no struggle. The selkie mother waited until she knew she was alone before placing the leather pelt back on and dove into the sea. When she found her children, they were asleep, dreaming pleasant dreams.

But the selkie discovered that she could not fall asleep herself. She lay awake in her seal form, watching the light dance in the waters, and thought of the human woman. She could have been cruel, but instead she had offered her food and warmth.

Why had she also been alone? What had happened to her family? What had happened to make her feel compassion towards a stranger, if only because it meant having company for a short time? Most importantly, why did the selkie mother wish to see her again?

She dared not return the next night, however. She did not want to raise her children's suspicions, or increase her own chances of being hurt again. She told herself it was for them. She told herself that she only wanted to make sure this woman was safe because it meant she could one day take her children to see her.

After that... perhaps, never again. A selkie never chose to stay on land. They would walk for a time and enjoy things they could not under the sea, such as fire, and cooking. But it was not their home. The only time a selkie lived a life on land was when their pelt was stolen and they had no choice. The selkie mother herself had been on land for nearly a year before she was finally presented with the chance of escape.

Yet now, times were different. She had three little children to care for. Only they were not so little anymore. Their time on land would come soon enough. Then would come the time when they would set off and make their own paths for their lives. What would she have, then?

Freedom.

She would have the freedom to wander the sea as she had before her children had been born. But she would also be alone. She supposed all that she wanted anymore was to feel safe. And the other night, when it had been her and that human woman, she had indeed felt safe.

A month went by before she felt brave enough to tempt more time on the land. Fortunately, her children did not find the idea to be strange. They believed it made sense for her to venture the world above to see that it was safe for them, after all.

That evening, after her children fell asleep, the selkie mother returned to the shores. When she had shed her leather pelt, she walked among the beaches until she came across the same woods as before. She entered them and wandered until she found a small fire, and the woman who had lit it.

She turned to the selkie mother and smiled. "I had been hoping you would find me again,"

Even though the selkie mother did not know what she was saying, she liked to hear the sound of the woman's voice. It was soft and soothing. She took a seat next to the woman, who produced two fish from a basket and began to cook them. The selkie mother closed her eyes and took in both sound and smell, as she inhaled deeply.

When the fish had finished, the two of them ate, and all was well. Too soon, it felt, the selkie mother realized she had consumed her meal, yet she did not feel the urgency to return to her children. In fact, she very much wanted to stay with the woman. If only for a little while longer.

Feeling bolder, she moved closer to the woman. The woman did not move away. The selkie thought perhaps she hadn't noticed. Did she want the woman to notice? Curious, she moved in even closer, and this time, the woman did respond. She reached out and wrapped an arm around the selkie.

"I know, " she said. "I am, too."

She rested her head on the woman's shoulder, and the two of them sat there and watched the fire dance. Eventually the embers died out and the sun began to peek between the trees. With a heavy sigh, the selkie stood up. The woman did not grab at her this time. She let her arm fall down as the selkie left her embrace. She had tears in her eyes.

Something was breaking inside of the selkie mother. She had felt this way before, the first time she had been on land, but it was different. That time, she had felt like a part of her had been stolen. Now, she felt as though she was hurting herself. She did not have time to dwell on it, however. She had to get back to her children.

The next few days, the selkie seemed to be in a trance. She wondered if this aching feeling would ever go away. Or was this part of her forever? She thought about how she had felt before she met the woman. How she still had these feelings, but they were duller. She only felt them so strongly now because the woman had also made her so happy.

Maybe it would be best not to see her again. She should focus on her children. And wait for them to grow up. Maybe then she would find happiness.

A month passed, and then another. On and on time went until a year had come and gone. The selkie mother found that her children had grown, and they were ready to see the world. She brought them to the shores. Her pelt came off easily, but it took much longer for her children, since it was their first time. She waited with great patience for them to take on their human forms.

They stumbled when they tried to walk. One stretched out their arms to hold balance, and the other two held onto each other's hands as they placed one foot in front of the other. Then they made their way over to their mother, and she led them from the beaches and into the forest.

"Why are we going into the woods, mother?" Asked her firstborn. "Is the town not safe for us?"

"No," the selkie mother insisted. "It is still too dangerous..."

Her firstborn nodded, but they seemed unconvinced. The selkie mother kept her eyes peered for the familiar fire. She acknowledged that it had been a year since she had last seen the woman, but she had rather hoped that, by some small miracle, she would still be waiting.

She didn't know what she would do once she found the woman. She didn't know how to explain the situation to her children. Nothing had happened, not really. She was just the only human the selkie felt safe with. That was all her children needed to know.

The four of them continued on their journey until at last there was a pillar of smoke. The selkie mother felt such relief at the sight, she ran towards it with no regards to her children following. They called after her and tried to catch up, but she did not hesitate. She brushed passed the trees until they opened up, and there she saw — not her woman, but a man.

He looked over and saw her standing there unclothed. She wanted to run, but her fear held her in place. Her children reached her, yet she did not have the strength to warn them off. The man surveyed the lot of them.

"I know what you are!"

They did not know his words, but they understood his meaning when he pointed at them. From behind, he produced a large fishing net. The family of selkies screamed as he began to chase them. The selkie mother wished she had never taken her children up. They all should have stayed in the sea, forever safe. Now, they would all be held prisoner, or worse.

Just then, the man gave out a resounding cry, and the selkie mother turned around to see a spear sticking out from his arm. The woman — her woman — came out from the trees and ran towards the man. She pulled out her weapon with one quick yank, causing the man to shriek out once more.

"Leave them!" The woman roared.

"Don't you know what they are?" The man asked in a strained voice. He knelt down and clutched at his wound. "They are selkies! They don't belong in this world!"

"They are not your concern!" The woman bellowed once more. The selkie mother had never seen something so powerful in all her life. "Leave at once! This is your final warning, or I will kill you!"

The man did not argue then. He took his net and left. Then the woman turned towards the family of selkies. She smiled, but there was a pained expression in her eyes. The same as the last time they had met. She nodded towards them, and turned to make her leave.

Now the selkie mother did something she never had before. She called out a word.

"W-wait...!"

This made the woman stop in her tracks. She faced the family, and they approached her slowly. The children were very hesitant, but their mother encouraged them. They circled around the woman, taking in her sight and her scent, until finally the firstborn stepped in and pressed a hand to the woman's shoulder. She smiled at the selkie youth, and pressed her own hand over the grasp. The rest of them embraced her.

The selkie mother felt something deep inside. As though a harsh, unrelenting wound from within had at last closed over, and she was at peace.

Later that evening, the woman took the family back to her cabin, where she prepared a wonderful sea food stew for their dinner. The children played with their shadows in the light of the fire. The woman and the selkie mother sat next to each other, and watched them.

The following morning, the children woke up early, eager to go back to the sea. Their mother and the woman walked them to the shore, but when it came time for them to place their leather pelts back on, the selkie mother hesitated.

"Mother?" Her firstborn asked. "What's wrong?"

"I... I do not wish to return..." she admitted.

It was embarrassing, to be vulnerable like this. Particularly in front of her children. But her firstborn nodded, as though she had expected this answer.

"We are grown now," she replied. "We can watch over ourselves. We can keep each other safe."

The selkie mother looked at her with bewilderment. "I don't mean... it's not that I want to leave all of you, I just... wish to stay here."

"I know. But we want to return to the sea." Their siblings nodded in agreement.

"There will be dangers," their mother protested.

"As there will be here," the firstborn countered. "We have each other, and you have your woman. We shall be back."

The selkie mother wept, unable to handle how much her children had matured. Where had the time gone? She embraced them all one last time before they departed back into the sea.

Then the woman stepped up and gently placed a hand on the selkie mother's shoulder, and the two of them went home.

ABOUT THE AUTHOR

Angela was raised on a diet of gothic horror and fairytales. Her earliest memories are of putting together homemade picture books using copy paper and pencils. Now she moreorless does the same thing, but with technology.

She lives with her cats, birds and fish tanks.

www.ingramcontent.com/pod-product-compliance
Lightning Source LLC
LaVergne TN
LVHW070227170826
845679LV00035B/1785
9798995801702